Slinky Malinki, Early Bird

Lynley Dodd

Early one morning
when all were asleep,
Slinky Malinki
decided to creep
out of his bed
in the shadowy gloom,
and off on the prowl
by the light
of the moon.

Past the piano
and wickerwork chairs,
he silently padded
to climb up the stairs.

'WRRROW?'
he said,
as he slipped through each door
to wake up the family,
one, two, three, four.

He purred in their ears

and he pounced on their toes,

he bristled his whiskers
and tickled each nose.

'PESKY OLD SLINKY!'
the family moaned,
'You woke us TOO EARLY!'
they grumbled and groaned.
'PLEASE
leave us in peace
for an hour or two!'
But
Slinky Malinki knew
just
what
to
do.

He bounced like a ball

and he played hide and seek,

he sang yowly songs
and he smooched every cheek.

He tipped over lamps
and he sat on their heads,

until he had pestered them
out of their beds.

They mumbled and moaned
as they stomped down the stairs,
they grumbled and groaned
as they flopped into chairs,
'We wanted some PEACE
for an hour or two!'
But
Slinky Malinki knew
just
what
to
do.

He patiently waited
then,
turning instead,

Slinky Malinki went
straight
back
to
bed.

PUFFIN BOOKS
Published by the Penguin Group: London, New York, Australia, Canada, India,
Ireland, New Zealand and South Africa
Penguin Books Ltd, Registered Offices: 80 Strand, London WC2R 0RL, England

puffinbooks.com

First published 2012
Published in this edition 2014
001

Made and printed in China

ISBN: 978–0–723–28838–1